Ruby

Knights In White Satin 5

By

Sharon Emerick

Chapter 1

As Ruby rode away from her home she reflected on her life. She knew everyone would think she was jealous of her small brothers and sister, even Misty would be looked at. Only it wasn't them she envied it was her older sister. They were outgoing and could talk their way in and out of anything. Ruby really was grateful for the sword training, but Diamond, Sapphire, Topaz, and Amber always made all the decisions and just expected her to happily go along with it. She could never get them to listen to her ideas or see things her way. "I'm not really running away; I just want to see what I can do without someone else second guessing me." She said to herself. Then, the memory of the child growing inside her brought her back to reality.

As she rode through the night, Ruby let her memories carry her.

Diamond, fist born and as bright and sharp as her name implied. She could win almost any argument with almost anyone, not because of her looks but because she was smart as well as pretty. Once, when a visiting dignitary argued with their father, five-year-old Diamond stood up and informed him 'How and Why' his arguments were wrong and convinced him to see thing her way. Which was also her fathers' way. Then Diamond came up with the idea of becoming warriors. At first it had been for self-defense, then to defend the kingdom. It had been Diamond who convinced the Arms Master to train them, it hadn't been hard to talk the sisters into it. What did

take a lot of work, was
making the girls train when
every muscle in their bodies
screamed in protest
especially in the beginning.
Ruby giggled, as she
remembered the look on
their fathers' face when his
little princesses pulled very
real swords on his guards
and held their own against
them. His fear was replaced
by Pride, but the worry
never faded.

Ruby's' mind returned to
the present. The moon had
risen higher. It was time to
take a break and get some
rest. Ruby had one last
thing to do before she slept.

Grabbing scissors out of her pouch she began to cut her hair. It would be hard to find her without her hair giving her away and the servants clothes she had borrowed. Putting strands into the stream so no evidence of her presence or disguise could be found. Changing into her borrowed attire, Ruby placed her normal clothes in the bag she had brought and tied it on to her horse. Then before she could change her mind, she turned the horse towards the castle and smacked her rump. After the horse was on it's way

Ruby walked another mile through the middle of the water so she left no tracks anyone else could follow. Then she laid down and slept.

When she woke, she knew she couldn't stay there, it was too close to her home. Once again Ruby walked in the middle of the creek to prevent leaving tracks. Once again, her mind wondered back, Ruby's eyes filled with tears as she thought of Sapphire.

Sapphire, the one that really didn't care what others thought of her. Sapphire would say the thing others wouldn't or feared saying. When she brought Misty home, she dared any one to deny that Misty was her daughter. When Misty had been taken by mistake, the rage was downright Scary. At that moment even her family was afraid of her. The knights became a release for her pent-up emotions. Sapphire had excelled at the physical exertion. She got what she wanted, not because she was pretty or wheedled and whined to get it. No, she got it because she always never saw any reason why it wouldn't be hers. When the man that murdered her had been away from his King, he tried to get her angry. Only Sapphire saw through what he was trying to do and laughed at him and his lame attempts at making her mad. Thus, he lost his mind when she had shown him up. With his humiliation in full view, he ripped her open from behind killing her instantly. He lasted less than a minute, the Girls exacted instant revenge. The funeral almost cost the Kingdom the Knights in White Satin. Except they knew that if they disbanded Sapphire would have died for nothing. To honor her memory, the Knights in White Satin remained active.

Ruby's stomach growled loudly, bringing her back to her present situation. She found herself in a clearing before she could think there was a massive wild hog standing in front of her. She drew the sword, also borrowed to replace her more ornate one, and waited. The hog was predictable, it charged. Accidental clumsiness allowed her sword to pierce its tough hide while it tried to kill her with its tusk.

That night Ruby slept with a full belly and a small fire for warmth. The next morning. Ruby cut the tusk off the hog and left the carcass for the scavengers.

Ruby walked into the woods and meandered around until she found a path to follow. She wasn't sure if it was an animal path or a human one. Once again, she let her mind wonder, this time it rested on the twins. Topaz and Amber, identical in looks, way different in personalities.

Topaz, she was the thinker of the two. She

talked Amber into or out of all kinds of things. Once she convinced Amber that a monster lived in her room so they should change rooms because the monster didn't like Amber and would leave her alone. So, Amber had changed rooms, Topaz had rigged little surprises to spook her sister. It worked for almost a week. Then one day Amber caught Topaz coming out of the room. The practical jokes stopped. When Diamond and Sapphire had the idea to train in self-defense, Topaz had jumped at doing something so unheard of.

Amber on the other hand didn't really want to, until their father decided to put all his girls on the same hall as the Royal Suite so the guards wouldn't be spread out. Then she saw the usefulness of the suggestion. Ruby remembered that none of them had given her a choice, she was told to be ready to work hard. Yea, she was grateful now but then, not so much.

Chapter 2

Ruby realized she was walking into a small village. People were looking at her and she really couldn't blame them. Her hair, it didn't look anywhere near its vibrant color, it was a dirty dusty shade of brown. Her clothes were ripped and filthy.

Ruby wanted to get something to eat but first she had to sell the tusks. Yeah, she had money with her, but it would look suspicious especially the way she looked right now.

If she sold the tusks, then got food no one would be suspicious about the money's origins. Finding a blacksmith, she bargained with him for about an hour until he finally gave her a decent price for both tusks and an old nag, he was tired of feeding it.

Ruby had seen an Inn while searching for the blacksmith. Making her way back to it, she entered and ordered an evening meal. As she ate, she listened to the locals gossiping. "Yeah, I heard that they left everything. Just up and left." One old man said to his companion. "Yeah, it won't be long before some one goes in and steals the livestock and anything else not nailed down." "I'll tell you the truth if it wasn't so far from town, I'd live there myself. Only a two-day ride is too much for my old bones. My missus would kill me too. She loves living in town." From the gesturing the two were doing Ruby figured out which direction the farmhouse was. When she finished her meal Ruby turned her horse towards the abandoned land. After another night under the stars, she rode into the vacant farm.

The animals were in distress. The cows needed milked, fed, and watered. The chickens need fed and watered. The dog and four little bundles of fluff needed attention as well.

Ruby had never done any of this kind of work in her life, but she would have to learn if she was going to make her own way. First, she stabled her horse, then went to the closest cow. Finding a bucket and stool, she tried to remember what the servants had done at the castle. With a lot of trail and error and extremely patient cows she finally got a bucket of milk.

With a lot of trial-and-error Ruby had managed to learn the basics. Throwing all the eggs she found on the first day away she knew that tomorrow's eggs would be fresh.

She finally entered the house. It was fully furnished but needed cleaning. Searching around Ruby found soap and after a trip to the creek she washed and scrubbed the rest of the day away. Before going to bed Ruby checked on her horse and cows plus the chickens. Everything seemed fine.

That night the wolves howled, an owl asked, "Who?" Snug in her bed ruby listened to the night sounds and slipped unknowingly into a deep sleep.

The next morning, she woke to the cows begging to be fed and milked, the rooster crowing, her horse needed to be taken to the fenced pasture, as well as the cows. Ruby had never realized how much work the servants and others non royal workers had to do just to survive. She was learning. With her morning chores finished Ruby went to the creek and bathed for as long as she could, washing her clothes and bedding, hanging it all on bushes and low hanging limbs of trees to dry by afternoon she had gathered fresh eggs, boiled, and eaten them, then put the fresh linens on the bed. Then she fed and stabled the animals, ate more boiled eggs, and went to bed.

Chapter 3

After a month Ruby forgot other people existed. The only voice she heard was her own as she greeted and tended her animals.

The dog she had seen when she arrived finally decided to trust her and made herself at home in the cabin. Ruby never saw the fluff balls, but MaMa (which is what Ruby named her) acted like she didn't miss them. So, Ruby never bothered to look for them.

One morning the animals were restless, they acted

edgy and were nervous. As
she fed them and mucked
out the stalls the sunshine
disappeared behind a bank
of seriously dark clouds.
Thunder rumbled in the hills
behind the farm, lightening
lit the sky. Finishing her
chores in a hurry Ruby and
MaMa raced for the cabin.
Just as they entered the sky
opened and a torrent of rain
pummeled the dry ground.
Rivers of muddy water
flowed past the house for
what felt like hours. As it
slowed Ruby and MaMa
went to tend the animals.

Opening the barn door,
MaMa backed up, hackles

rising and a growl coming
from deep in her chest.
Listening, Ruby only heard
the soft sounds of contented
animals.   As her eyes
adjusted, a startled gasp
escaped her lips. There
were now two horses.
MaMa made straight for the
unused stall at the back of
the barn. Lips pulling back
in a menacing grin MaMa
pounced on a bundle of
straw. "Hey, call this Bitch
off already!" Instantly Ruby
had her sword in her hand.
"MaMa, Come!" MaMa
backed out of the stall never
taking her eyes off the man
as he unburied himself.

Sword at the ready Ruby confronted him, "WHO ARE YOU? AND WHAT ARE YOU DOING IN MY BARN?

"Whoa little Miss! Be careful with that toad sticker you could really hurt yourself." Ruby lifted it higher. "Ok, if that's the way you want it, I guess I'll have to teach you not to play with a sword." With this he unsheathed the sword he carried. "MaMa stay!" Was all Ruby said as she readied for his attack. When it came, he was not prepared for her response. As the fight continued, he grew more fearful. As rusty as she was Ruby was besting him. With a flip of her wrist Ruby stabbed him in the stomach. She watched as he breathed his last. With the help of his horse, she dragged his body to the woods for the wild creatures to feast on. Returning to the barn Ruby rubbed down her new horse, fed and tended to the rest of her livestock then her and MaMa returned to the house. Wet and tired, Ruby and MaMa retired for the night. MaMa curled up next to her and both soon were in dreamland.

The next morning the rain still fell only now it was a lot less torrential and more of a steady shower. After tending to her chores, Ruby decided it was time to find something else to eat besides eggs, her and MaMa were getting really tired of eggs. Luck was on her side. A deer had broken its leg and lay waiting to die. Thanking it for it's sacrifice Ruby put it out of its misery and using her horse towed the carcass back to the farm. Without a clue as to how to cut it up she chopped it up with the axe from the wood pile.

Throwing a hunk in a pan
she cooked her first real
meal. MaMa ate the
butchered scraps raw. With
her chores finished, Ruby
looked at her abused sword.
It needed cleaned and
sharpened, she also did the
knife hidden by a sheath
strapped on her leg.

As night settled in Ruby
went out and set on the
porch. Her hair had started
to grow long again. So, with
her scissors she once again
cut it. The intruder had
known she was female even
though she wore pants. It
had to be because of her
hair.

Each day was the same. Ruby got up took care of her critters and the house, then went in search of food. With MaMa's help there was squirrel, rabbit, and another deer. All the pieces that MaMa didn't eat returned to the wild to feed any in need.

Winter was on its way, the leaves were beginning to turn into lovely colors, MaMa's hair became thick. Ruby began looking for dead trees and branches, stacking it all in a lean to next to the house. Everyday she trekked farther from home. The horses could pull one or two fallen trees back to the farm. There she wacked and hacked them into useable pieces with the axe. MaMa was her constant companion and would hunt as Ruby collected her wood.

Ruby's belly rounded and grew, the baby kicked and moved constantly. Names came and went thru her mind. For a boy, she was thinking Quentin, a girl, Angelique. She'd lost track of when she was due. The weather grew chill and crisp. Winter was closer than she had thought. On nice days the horses and cows enjoyed the pasture.

The chickens roosted more
and layed fewer eggs. Time
meant nothing to Ruby. Her
days were filled with
chores, her nights
exhaustion.

Chapter 4

Then one morning she could barely get out of bed. Her backache so bad, standing up straight was impossible. The most she could do was let MaMa out and returned to her bed. Ruby's moans soon escalated to screams. Somewhere in her nightmare of pain a soft voice spoke. "Easy sweet girl, you're gonna be just fine." Ruby didn't know how but the voice was calm and gentle. "Here we go, now push, this will soon be over.

Push!" The calm command of the stranger's voice eased her fears as she pushed. The voice counted one, two, three one more push, atta girl. Ruby heard a slap and the wail of a baby. Smiling she began to relax when she was hit with another wave of pain. Once again, the voice talked her through, one, two, three push. Another slap and a weaker cry answered. "Congratulations Sweetheart! It's twin. One boy and One girl. When your awake enough you can give me their names and yours too." With a laugh the voice left the room. MaMa jumped up to lay next to her and Ruby slept.

The next morning Ruby woke with her breasts swollen but feeling much better. Looking down she realized her belly was flat. Finding clean rags, she used them to gather her blood. Hearing whimpers and a soft voice soothingly talking, she entered the other room. A huge man with red hair and green twinkling eyes stood above her babies, MaMa lay at his feet. Ruby walked to him. "I owe you, Thanks Sir." "You owe your wolf the Thanks. She came to my

camp and wouldn't take no
for an answer. She
basically herded me here, I
found you in hard labor. She
almost took my leg off when
I went to get water." He
laughed. It was a wonderful
sound. Bending over, Ruby
rubbed her best friend's
belly. "Thanks MaMa." "I
like her name it fits her.
She sure looked after you
like a MaMa. Oh, speaking
of names I'm Sean O'Malley
and you are?" "Ruby."
"Alright lass now do these
wee ones have name?"
Lying snuggled together
were two perfect but tiny
babes. "The boy is Quentin;

the girl is Angelique." Ruby replied. Both babies cooed. "Oh, I milked the cows and fed them from a calf bottle I found in the barn. Whoa sweet girl, I washed it in the creek first." As he saw her getting ready to explode. "Well, I need to get back to my camp. Who is helping you keep this farm up?" Ruby pointed to MaMa. "I know it's not my business but where is there father?" Ruby hung her head. "Dead." Was the only answer she gave. "Miss Ruby, I need a place to stay for the winter. I will work for my keep and help with

the wee ones too."
Realizing she was definitely
going to need help through
the winter Ruby agreed.
"Alright Sweet Girl, I'll break
down my camp and be back
soon." After he left Ruby
realized how empty her
home was.

     She did laundry and put
fresh diapers on the babies,
nursed them and put a slab
of meat on the stove for
herself. As the day drew to
a close Ruby wrapped the
tiny people and laid them in
a feed trough, she had found
hidden in a spare room she
hadn't seen. Once it was
cleaned and clean bedding

was placed in it, she had a perfect bed for Quentin and Angelique.

Putting her knife on and clean trousers a clean shirt and her sword Ruby felt like her old self again. As she tended to the animals that relied on her she felt more than saw MaMa bristle. A snarl came from outside the barn door. The horses became skittish, the cows were a little calmer but not by much. Drawing her sword, she worried that another man had come upon her farm. A paw the size of her face slashed under the door. Ruby had never seen

a live bear; she was about
to meet one soon. Grabbing
a pitchfork, she waited. Her
sword was back in its
scabbard. The pitchfork
gave her a longer reach.
Mama paced; Ruby stood
her ground. Another paw,
and another scoop of dirt
making the hole under the
barn door bigger and
deeper. A snout appeared;
MaMa stated forward.
"MaMa NO!" Ruby walked to
the door and rammed the
tines of the pitchfork into
the bear's nose. The bear
pulled back and roared its
anger. With fury it hit the
barn doors, they buckled but

still stood. Once again, the
bear rammed the doors.
This time they cracked. The
horses panicked, the cows
milled restlessly and bawled
their fear. Once again, the
door was bombarded this
time it gave. Rising to its
two feet the bear advanced,
MaMa attacked. Ruby
watched as her friend would
go in and harass then back
off. After she get the
rhythm of Mama's attacks
she used the pitchfork
effectively, with a final
thrust she watched as the
bear dropped to all fours.
Bleeding heavily the bear
advanced on the horses.

With a scream of fury Ruby
buried the pitchfork into the
stubborn enemy.

Suddenly another dog
appeared as well as Sean.
Both took over the fight.
MaMa stood in front of Ruby
while Sean and his dog
finished off the bear. Once
they were sure it was dead
Sean came over to make
sure Ruby was alright. "Are
you hurt? How long you
been fighting that beast?"
With the fight over Ruby
began to shake. Sean
wrapped his massive arms
around her, picked her up
and carried her to the
house. "You rest now, that

"Well, Mornin sweet girl.
Sit, eat then let's talk."
Sean said.

Chapter 5

"I did a bit of exploring while you were sleeping and found a room over there." He pointed to the spare room she had found the trough in. "I thought Bear and I could make that our room for the winter. I also have a question about how you learned to use that sword. You are exceptional with it. We have all winter to get to know each other. Also, we need a few things from town, like pots and pans, more soap, flour, anything else you can think

of?" With a soft smile Ruby
went into her room and
returned with a small bag of
coins. "Blankets, maybe a
wagon? Anything you think
we'll need and yes that
backroom is all yours.
Whatever you need to fix it
up. Oh, and you'll need a
bed, I don't know what you'll
need but this should get
most of our needs." "No, No
I have a little money, I can
get what I need without
using your savings." "You
are doing me a favor by
going into town, so I don't
have to drag Quentin and
Angelique out in the
weather. Let me do this."

With a sigh he took her
money and they prepared for
him to leave the next day.
There was a debate whether
Bear should stay at the farm
or travel with Sean. "I have
MaMa, you need Bear to
guard your back. Take him
with you. I'll feel better."
With a nod Sean conceded.

After Sean had left Ruby
took care of the livestock.
She put the horses in the
pasture, milked the cows
and checked the barn door
that he had patched
together the night of the
bear attack. Even tho they
both hated waste, Sean had
placed nails pointing

downward to discourage
anything from digging under
again. Even so she never
went to the barn without her
sword and MaMa, the knife
strapped to her leg.

Her days went by quickly
between the animals and
the twins. At night she
cleaned the spare room. It
was a treasure trove,
candles, matches, and
lanterns. All kinds of
clothes, blankets, things
she had no clue as to what
they were. She hoped that
by the time Sean returned
the room would be clean
and ready for him. Before
he had shown up Ruby had

never realized how totally isolated, she was. Now she felt it. One day ran into the next. She lost track of time, but the weather didn't. Leaves fell, the wind carried a chill and night arrived earlier every day.

Ruby worked harder than ever. Keeping wood in the cabin, the barn mucked out, chickens put inside for convenience.   Her weapons were cleaned and sharpened; it was getting too cold to wash diapers in the creek. Then one morning Ruby woke to the sounds of pellets hitting the cabin. It was sleeting, not

just a little bit but a
continuing background
music to her routine. After
carefully tending the
animals in the barn Ruby
made her way back to the
cabin. The twins were
gurgling and sort of chirping
to each other. Finally, Ruby
got ready for bed. Once
again, she forgot there were
other people in the world.

She woke to MaMa
whining, running from the
door to her room. Grabbing
her sword, she crept to the
door and listened. A jiggling
and an animal's snort, then
a dog's bark. Throwing
open the door MaMa ran out

barking and jumping for joy. Bear met her halfway. "Hey Sweet Girl, let me get the wagon in the barn and I'll be right in." With a wave Ruby went back to the cabin to wait.

Putting more wood in the stove Ruby cooked a slab of meat, so Sean could have a warm meal when he got inside. Heavy footsteps on the porch announced he was ready to come inside, with a smile Ruby let him in. With Bear and MaMa, he entered. "Sorry Sweet Girl, I know it's been over a month, but I got caught up doin' some trading. I bought something that someone else needed, they traded for something else we needed, and it just kept on. I lost track of the days. We can bring everything inside in the morning.

Bear made a beeline to the trough containing the sleeping twins, after giving each a lick him and MaMa moved closer to the stove. Ruby served Sean his meal and Bear got the scraps. "I just figured you had found a new place to spend the winter." Ruby said with a shrug. "MaMa and I went on with our routine." Coming up behind her Sean put his hands on her shoulders. "I wouldn't do that to you Sweet Girl, let alone those helpless babies." Ruby yawned. "Well talk more after we get some sleep." "Good Night." As she slid into sleep Ruby realized just how happy she was.

When she woke, she smelt food and heard the soft crooning Sean always did for the twins. Ruby knew she had found her home; it wasn't the farm completely it was the farm and Sean. After they ate the two went out to the barn.

Sean showed Ruby all the things he had bartered

and bought. There were coats, boots, and a butter churn. Spices, salt, pepper, and flour. He had also found a way to get a wagon and feed for the chickens. She showed him the empty spare room and the treasures she had found when they finished their chores. Then with the old wood found in the barn, they built Sean a bed.

Their days blended together. They talked and laughed, argued, and cried. Life was good.

Ruby was content.

Chapter 6

Winter arrived full strength. Sean and Ruby had prepared as much as possible. Rope had been strung from the barn door to the cabin door in case of a blizzard, extra wood was gathered at every opportunity. Sean hunted, Ruby learned to cook other things then boiled eggs and slabs of meat. The twins were growing and giggling more and more. MaMa began action strange. Bear would try to snuggle up with her and she growled and ran him off their bed.

Sometime in the night the blizzard they had prepared for arrived. The winds whistled through hidden cracks; snow piled up on the porch. MaMa refused to leave the stove, Bear would go to the barn with them using them to guide him back and forth while they clung to the rope.

On the second morning of unrelenting snow Ruby and Sean both were woken by soft mewling's. During the night Mama gave birth to three tiny replicas of herself and three little Bears. Her

tail thumped the floor as
they admired her babies.
Bear wouldn't leave the
house so Ruby, and Sean
got the chores completed as
usual and were returning
when Ruby felt the rope
slacken. Pulling herself to
the door and opening it,
Bear almost knocked her
over as he ran out on to the
porch. With a giant leap he
surged into the deep snow,
MaMa wasn't far behind him.
Both dogs began searching,
they were frantic.

Ruby stocked the stove
and paced. After 15
minutes she heard heavy
slow steps approaching the

door. When it opened Sean and both dogs entered. "What happened?" "I thought I heard something behind me, I guess I dropped the rope when I turned around." "What was it your heard?" "I couldn't see or hear anything. Until Bear and MaMa found me, I was completely lost."

The next morning the sunshine made the snow glisten with a million rainbows. The twins were so active that Ruby and Sean bundled them up and carried them to the barn.

When they opened the door, they were greeted by

cows already milked, chickens fed, stalls cleaned, and horses fed and content. Looking at each other Ruby, Sean, and the babies entered. Drawing her sword Ruby poked into haystacks and around anything that could hide someone. "Ouch came from a pile of muck when she poked it. A boy stepped out from the muck pile in his arms he held a tiny little girl. Ruby gasped. Bear ran to them, giving both his approval with a quick lick. Sean stood with his hands on his hips. "So, I did hear something last night." He said. Did you do all this?" Gesturing to the finished barn! "Yea it was my way of paying back for my little sister and I staying here." "Where are your parents?" With a shake of his head the boy conveyed that they were deceased. When the blizzard started, they laid over us to keep us safe. They died the first night. We've been moving around trying to find a cave or somewhere to sleep. We stumbled on your farm last night. I was awake early, so I took care of your animals. Oh, we also drank some of your milk. We don't have any money, but I'll work to pay for it." This reminded everyone the cabin was warm and the two intruders were probably hungry.

"Teddy, I'm hungry" Before Teddy could reply Sean picked the little girl up. "So, the tiny mouse has a voice. What's your name mouse?" Giggling the girl said, "Ella" and that's my brober Teddy." Ruby picked up the twins and headed for the barn door. The boy came up and plucked Quentin into his own arms. "Since the big man is carrying Ella, I can help you carry these guys." Once outside they walked in a straight line to the cabin. Bear rushed to greet MaMa and the pups. After everyone was inside Ruby and Sean began cooking. "Ted, we think you should stay with us. It is safer especially for Ella. You did a magnificent job keeping her alive, but the weather can get meaner as winter goes on. By the way how old are you two?" Teddy stood up taller with the praise. "I'm 12 and Ella is four almost five. We don't accept charity." "Oh, you can help alright. You did a great job this morning. It'll be good to have another man around the house."

After they ate Ruby began churning butter while the twins toddled around. Ted began to frantically looking around. "What's wrong Ted?" Ruby asked. "I can't find Ella. I've looked everywhere." MaMa came and sat beside Ruby. Forlornly eyeing her bed. On a hunch Ruby went to take a peek, sure enough snuggled in with the six pups was one tiny girl, fast asleep. She had pushed MaMa out. Putting her finger on her lips she led Ted to where he could see his sister.

Sean and Ted spent the rest of the day cutting wood, clearing the porch, and making the rope from the barn door to the house more secure.

Chapter 7

Winter held it's grip tightly for months. Then trees budded green showed through the slush and the sun stayed out longer and longer.

Sean surprised Ruby with seeds for a garden. Him and Ted prepared a plot, planted it.

The horses enjoyed the pasture and Sean, and Ted went looking for a bull. Life was good.

The twins and Ella played in the sun with MaMa and

the pups while Ruby cleaned and tended to the everyday maintenance. During the evenings Sean and Ruby taught Ted to use a sword and bow and arrow. Ella tried; she was better with the knife. Quentin and Angelique were still too easily distracted to be trusted with sharp items. Ted excelled at the sword and bow and arrow not so well with the knife. He didn't like the up-close fighting. Ella on the other hand preferred the knife but became quite good with the bow and arrow as well.

One day Sean came up to Ruby and asked if they could talk after the kids were in bed. Ruby worried all day about what he was going to say. She was so nervous she spilt milk, almost took her toe off hoeing their newly planted garden. Finally, dinner was done, training over and some very tired kids tucked in and asleep. Sean put his arm around her waist and escorted her outside to the porch.

"When are you leaving?" She asked. "You have stayed here out of pity I know." With a look of complete confusion on his face Sean replied.

"Leaving? I'm not leaving unless you want me to. I wanted to ask you if you would marry me. Before you say I don't know anything about you. I have a secret; I've known all along who you are princess. Not many women can handle a sword and knife like you do. It was easy to put two and two together. I have fallen in love with you. Watching you take every hardship and every blessing with a smile and pride. So, will you? Marry me I mean." With a squeal of delight Ruby jumped into his arms. "You're not leaving me? I love you so much I didn't know how I could handle you living somewhere else. Yes, yes, I'll marry you." Walking to the barn the two confirmed their love.

Returning to the cabin, the two made plans. While Ruby cleaned and prepared the two bedrooms, Sean, and Ted built beds for the kids. The room that Sean had used was too small for four beds sitting side by side but by stacking them all four would have their own bed. Ladders were placed beside the top beds.

Boys on one side, Girls on other. Ted got his choice of top beds. Quentin would be below him. Ella could climb the ladder only they worried about her rolling out and falling. So, Ted and Sean made a removable barrier to prevent that.

Ruby was making breakfast when she heard a tiny voice behind her. "Mommy we're hungry." Ella stood with the twins, "where's Ted and Daddy?" She knew they wouldn't eat until everyone was there. "Out in the barn sweetheart. Do you and the twins want to go get them?" With giant grins the three raced for the door. "Dad, Ted come in and eat. We're hungry!" Ruby laughed.

The high-pitched scream came from one of the three. Ruby was out the door in what felt like the blink of an eye. Sean and Ted came from the barn at a full Run. Bear and MaMa were standing in front of the toddlers snarling at the intruder. A cougar, big and eyeing the children hungrily, pacing. Bear and MaMa both attacked, distracting it while Sean, Ted, and Ruby each grabbed a child and headed for the house. When the children were safe the three defenders went to help the dogs. The cat had fled. MaMa lay on her side, Bear standing over her in case the cat returned.

Carefully Sean picked her up and carried her to her favorite bed, by the stove. That night MaMa crossed the Rainbow Bridge. Sean, Ruby, and Bear buried her before the kids got up. Ruby cried; MaMa was the first friend she had made. The pups, like MaMa's earlier pups had disappeared. While the kids ate breakfast Sean and Ruby told them that MaMa had died, they all cried. Then Ruby told them she was going to have a baby in the spring.   Sean and Ted began adding on to the house.

Chapter 8

It had been almost three years since Ruby had seen her family. On a whim she wrote a letter to her parents. Sean paid a man in town to deliver it. In it she explained that they couldn't leave the farm unattended so she wasn't sure when they would visit.

The baby arrived in the middle of the night. He was a beautiful healthy boy with a great set of lungs. Once again, the trough was put to good use. They named him after Sean's father, Harry.

He was the children's responsibility. They watched over him. Ella had taken to wearing her knife since the cougar, she stood guard almost as well as MaMa had. Quentin and Angelique had improved immensely with their weapons. Both were becoming excellent swordsmen. Knives were fast and accurate, Ella still bested them. Even Ted was impressed with her.

Once again Ruby was expecting. Nine months later, Poppy made her presence known. Life became busier than ever.

The cows were calving, the
horses had foals.

Sean had gone into town;
Ted had stayed to protect
the farm. Usually, the two
were inseparable. This time
even Bear had stayed. It
had been a week, Ruby and
Ted tended the farm and
garden while the youngster
played.

Ruby would stop and
listen if she heard anything
that sounded like the horse
and wagon. Ted kept
glancing down the lane.

The next morning Bear
woke everyone in the house
up. His barking was happy,

and his tail was wagging hard. Ruby heard the jingling of bridles and the squeak of wagon wheels. She rushed to the door. Ted yelled, "DAD'S HOME!" All the children rushed to greet him. With the kids and Bear crushing him, Sean fell to the ground laughing.

Ruby walked over and offered her hand to help him up. A squeal came from the back of the wagon. A little pink head peeked from a box. "I bought some pigs, that's what took me so long getting back. I had to go get them. Then the male got loose and ran off. I kept the sow by tying her to a tree. She gave birth to that little cutie this morning." With in an hour a pig pen had been built and fresh grass placed in as a bed for the momma pig and her now eight babies.

That night everyone laughed and celebrated Sean's safe return. Sean and Ruby left the kids in the cabin playing while they tended to the chores. The night was peaceful and quiet, the moonlight soft after the harsh sun.

Autumn was approaching fast, once again Sean, and Ted began stock piling

wood. The garden gave up
the last of its crops. Ruby
and the children saved as
many seeds as possible,
then tilled the ground for the
coming summer.

Winter arrived before all
the leaves had fallen. It
arrived in the middle of the
night with rain, and sleet.
Getting the pigs into the
barn was dangerous and
hilarious. Sean slipped and
landed on his butt while
holding two of the piglets.
Ruby was laughing so hard
she missed her step and
landed on her butt next to
him.

On a night of a Blizzard, Bear passed away in his sleep. The family mourned him and MaMa.

The rope was once again put up between the barn and the house. The children became cranky at being stuck inside, Sean and Ruby would get into arguments. Things were tense. When a scratching and whining at the door caught all of their attention. When they cracked the door open a tiny puppy crawled in. It immediately became the focus of the family, Ruby warmed up some broth and Sean towel dried it. "She's

a girl." Sean proclaimed.
She fit in the palm of his
hand. "How did she
survive? Where did she
come from?" These
questions had no answers.
Ruby looked at everyone
and said, "May I name her?"
All eyes focused on her.
"Warrior." The pup, fed and
warm, slept through it all.

Chapter 9

Spring arrived. Warrior never grew any Bigger, but her attitude remained Bigger than her. She herded the cattle as well as any dog three time her size, she stood her ground and protected all when there was a threat.

As the day grew longer life became busier and more relaxed at the same time. Sean and Ted cut and split wood, Ruby planted a garden, and the children did spring clean up around the

yard. No one was unarmed
except Harry and Poppy.

Then one day there was
a racket from the road.
Stepping out on to the porch
as a contingent of Knights
approached all in White
Satin. At the head sat King
Ronald and Queen Veronica,
Ruby almost fainted.
Warrior growled and barked
at the strangers. Sean
stepped up beside Ruby.
"Do you know these people
Sweet Girl?" "It's my
Family!" She said as she
ran to her parents.

Ronald and Veronica
stepped off their steads and
embrace her. In no time she

was surrounded and hugged. Everyone talking at once. Finally, Sean interrupted. "We need to get things arranged." For instance, where everybody is going to sleep, dinner and feed for the animals." By this time what looked like a moving town arrived. "We brought our own accommodations," Ronald stated.

Finally, after the tents were put up and dinner which Ronald's servants cooked and served, Ruby had a chance to introduce her family to her family. "Mom, Dad, Brothers, and Sisters this is my husband

Sean," wrapping her arm around his waist. "These monsters," she said with a grin, "are our children, Ted, Ella, Quentin, Angelique, Harry, and Poppy. Oh, and least I forget our ferocious dog, Warrior." Everyone fussed over the tiny terror, oh I mean terrier. All the kids were herded outside. The house was full, the yard was full, and the pasture overflowed with livestock.

Ruby and Sean Had nothing to do, Wood was being cut and split, the house was cleaned, and the garden maintained by her parents' servants, self-defense was taken over by all the cousins. Even Harry and Poppy were being given lessons.

Diamond, Topaz, and Amber, all gossiped about people she used to know. Catching her up on people that she didn't care about.

Her Mother and Father asked her to come home with them. "No! This is My home." "You can't be happy here. You have nothing, no servants, a tiny house, I mean there isn't enough room for all of you."

Ruby stood up. "Enough! I moved here because I can

be who I want to be. I don't
care now or then about all
the nonsense that comes
with being royal. My family
and I have a good life here.
Our children are happy and
responsible. If you aren't
happy here, as much as I
love and Miss you all, You
Can Leave!" Ruby was
furious.

Before any more could be
said, Warrior was barking
frantically, the kids were
yelling, and more noise
came from outside. Another
caravan of travelers pulled
into the yard.

Sean was excited. His
father arrived. Once again

space was wangled for more tents. The pasture was overflowing. Introductions were made and everyone settled.

Soon the hunters were hunting, and more wood was being cut and burned. The barn was cleaned and repaired. The animals were tended to by everyone but Ruby and her family. The kids were getting plenty of training, just not from Sean and Ruby. The house was expanded. No one asked the owners, Ruby, and Sean, how they wanted it. It was just done.

A run to town was made by a servant, he came back with a new wood stove to help heat the new addition, food, and other supplies.

Ruby and Sean watched as the surplus wood they would need for the upcoming winter was depleted.

One day ted came over to talk to them. "Mom, Dad, when is everyone leaving? It's been a month and we want out home back." He said gesturing to his brothers, and sisters. "We loved having them but now they act like the farm isn't good enough and they want

to go home. Plus, our wood
and hay aren't going to last
the winter if they don't leave
soon." "We know Ted, we
are watching." Ruby
replied. "Our supplies are
banishing, and fall is just
around the corner. We'll
work it out. I love them but
once again they are second
guessing everything I want.
I have never been happier.
They just won't see that!"
A figure slowly walked away
from where she had been
watching and listening.

The next day Queen
Veronica came up to Ruby
and said, "Honey are you
sure you don't want to come

back with us?" "No Mom, my life is here and I'm happy, so are Sean and the kids."

"Warrior, what's wrong?" As she looked at the tiny dog. Warrior waddled over to a small terrier and laid down next to him. "Where did you come from?" Ruby asked. "Is he yours Mom?" "No, I've never seen it before." She answered. "Well, it seems we have a new addition." Ruby said as she bent over to pick up the little dog. Sean took one look and laughed. "Another one?" "Yep." Ruby answered.

That night Ronald declared that it was time to call their visit over. "We've been here a month. It's time to return home. We'll be ready to leave by the end of the week." During the remaining time they stayed, wood was gathered, trips to town, where shoes and coats were bought. Blankets were purchased for all the new beds, they had made. Hay and feed were boughten from the struggling farmers in the area.

By the end of the week the tents were gone and the yard and pasture considerably emptier. Sean's dad was making his own arrangements. Unknown to Ruby or Sean, Harry had had a separate but attached cabin built on to their home. "I have no reason to return to my old home. Your brothers can handle the affairs there. I want to stay and spend time with you two and my grandkids." "Winter are rough out here dad! Are you sure?" "I sure am, and besides soldier would never forgive me taking him from Warrior."

Soldier hearing his name lifted his head. "So that's

his name! The kids have tried. Everything." Sean said smiling. "Yeah, I've had him a few months." Everyone settled for the night. The silence was heavenly.

Chapter 10

Winter once again came in strong. Once again, the rope was attached to the barn. Life returned to normal.

When spring returned, a lone man arrived with a note from Ruby's parents.

Ruby, Sean, and family,
    We would like to visit again. We had a very enjoyable time. We will not make this yearly. Looking forward to next year.
                Love You All,
                You Mom and Dad

With a sigh of relief, they sent their answer. Assuring that they would enjoy it.

As the kids got older, they would travel to visit everyone. Ruby and Sean looked forward to all of it.

Harry lived a very long life. Sean's brothers would come visit. And stay a week and return to their homes.

Ruby looked around at her life. She had everything. She was at peace.

The End